The Legend of PINKFOOT

By Mary Tillworth
Illustrated by MJ Illustrations
Cover illustration colored by Steve Talkowski

Teleplay "The Legend of Pinkfoot" by Janice Burgess

A Random House PICTUREBACK® Book

Random House 🏠 New York

randomhouse.com/kids
ISBN 978-0-385-38411-7
MANUFACTURED IN CHINA
10 9 8 7 6 5 4 3 2 1
Glow effect and production: Red Bird Publishing Ltd., U.K.

Deema was on her way to school one morning when she met a Crab Scout leader with three of his scouts. They had just woken up and were coming out of their tents.

"Good morning, Deema!" said the Crab Scout leader, stretching his claws.

Deema waved. "Hi! Did you sleep here all night?"

He nodded. "Sure did!"

"We're camping," a little Crab Scout explained.

"We set up our tents and ate dinner around a campfire," added another Crab Scout. "And then we all sat around the fire and heard a spooky story called 'The Legend of Pinkfoot.'"

"I like spooky stories! I want to go camping!" Deema exclaimed.

Deema swam excitedly to school to meet her friends. "I saw some Crab Scouts. They were out camping!"

"What's camping?" asked Goby.

"Camping is like a sleepover outside," explained Nonny.

"You get to tell spooky stories around a campfire," Deema added. "I LOOOOVE spooky stories!"

"What else do you do when you go camping?" asked Oona.

"Let's think about it," said Mr. Grouper. "When you sleep outside, you stay warm in a . . ."

"Sleeping bag!" answered Gil.

"Right!" said Mr. Grouper. "And when you go camping, you gather around the fire to roast . . ."

"Marshmallows!" said Molly. "Then you can make s'mores! Yummy!"

The Bubble Guppies decided to play camping right in the classroom. Oona, Gil, and Goby put their building blocks on sticks and pretended they were roasting marshmallows for s'mores.

As they sat around a pretend fire, Goby began to tell a spooky story.
"This is called 'The Legend of Pinkfoot,'" he said in a ghostly voice. "It's
the story of a giant pink shrimp who lives in the woods and likes to eat
s'mores. His name is . . . Pinkfoot."

"We should hear this story around a real campfire," said Mr. Grouper.
"Anybody want to go camping?"
"Yay!" cheered the Bubble Guppies.

The Bubble Guppies packed up their camping gear, and soon they were on their way to a campsite in the woods. As the sun went down and the full moon rose, they sang songs by the fire and roasted marshmallows for s'mores.

Finally, it was time for Goby's spooky story. The Bubble Guppies gathered close as he began. "Legend has it that if you go camping when the moon is full and you make s'mores, then Pinkfoot might come." Goby's voice dropped. "And if he does . . ."

"Then what happens?" asked a strange voice. Deema turned to see a huge pink shrimp sitting next to her!

"Pinkfoot!" Deema shouted.

Pinkfoot nodded and put a finger to his lips. "Shhh. Goby's not finished with his story!"

Goby smiled. "And if you give Pinkfoot a s'more, he'll sing a song for you!"

He handed Pinkfoot a s'more. Pinkfoot gobbled it down, then leapt onto a log and began to sing.

"Gracias for the story;
Many thanks for the snack!
Each time you make s'mores,
I'm sure to come back!

"If you roast your marshmallows
By the light of the moon
And make s'mores for Pinkfoot,
Then I'll come to you soon.
I'll come to you sooooon!"

It was a great song—and a great campout!